Look up into the sky. Can you see the rainbow? It arches like a bridge over the hills and comes down into Nutshell Wood. At the end of the rainbow, deep in the wood, a tiny magical village is appearing. That village is Rainbow's End. Rainbow's End can only be seen by humans when a rainbow is in the sky, otherwise it is invisible to everyone except the gnomes who live there and the woodland animals.

The gnomes of Rainbow's End are jolly little folk who are always busy. Lots of exciting and interesting things happen in the village and no one is ever bored. This book tells the story of something that happened there. A little bird told me!

Rainbow's End

A Trip to Granny Rumbletummy's

Written by Jane Patience
Illustrated by John Patience

This 1987 edition published by Derrydale Books,
Distributed by Crown Publishers Inc.,
225 Park Avenue South, New York, N. Y. 10003.
© Peter Haddock Ltd: Rainbow's End Productions.
Printed in Hungary

ISBN 0-517-64963-2

It was dusk in Rainbow's End, the time of day just before it goes dark, when the bats are out sweeping and swerving just above your head, catching insects. On the village green, Billy Hornblower raised the ancient horn to his mouth and blew a long deep note that rang out loud and clear in the woods all around. The job of Hornblower was a very old and very important one, and Billy's father had done it before him, and his father before him. The horn was blown at dusk each evening to guide travellers and gnomes, who were working out in the woods, back to the town before dark.

When Billy got home he hung up his jacket behind the kitchen door and the horn on its special hook above the fireplace. Then he saw that his sister Poppy and brother Sam were both tucked up on the settle by the fire, with a quilt covering their knees. They both looked very pale and miserable. "What's the matter with you two?" Billy asked. "Oh, they've both caught a nasty cold," their mother said as she came bustling in with a tray of steaming mugs. "If they're no better in the morning, I'll send you to see Granny Rumbletummy, Billy."

The next morning, Sam and Poppy were still poorly, so Billy set off to Granny Rumbletummy's house. The old lady wasn't really Billy's Grandmother, but everybody called her that because she was so old. She lived all alone in a cottage on the other side of the Tale Water, which was a swift flowing stream running through a steep, narrow gorge. Granny was a wise woman and knew all about the herbs that grew in the woods and made medicines from them. Now, there was a perfectly good bridge that crossed the Tale Water, but like other small boys, Billy Hornblower much preferred to take the short cut across a slippery old fallen tree which spanned the steep-sided gorge.

As Billy made his way across the moss-covered tree trunk, he suddenly slipped and fell. And that would have been the end of Billy Hornblower if his new red and yellow braces had not caught on a twig, leaving him dangling above the swirling waters below. As he hung there, hardly daring to move in case the braces should slip off the twig,

Billy remembered the horn which he had brought with him. It was really only supposed to be taken out of the house each evening for the Hornblowing on the village green, but Billy liked to carry it around with him because it made him feel important. Now he carefully lifted it to his lips and blew a long deep note.

After a few moments, Billy heard a rustling in the bushes on the other side of the gorge. Then a little, whiskered face appeared, then another. Rabbits! They looked at Billy and then disappeared. The two rabbits hopped off along a winding path through the trees, until they came to a pretty cottage in a clearing. It was Granny Rumble-tummy's house, and there she was in the garden, gathering herbs.

The rabbits explained what they had seen. ''Ah, yes,'' Granny said, ''I thought I heard the sound of the horn.'' Putting down her basket of herbs, she went into the cottage. Once inside, she hurried to an old carved blanket chest. She lifted the lid and rummaged around until she found what she wanted. ''Here we are,'' she muttered to herself as she held up a large and beautifully-patterned patchwork quilt. ''I think this will do.'' With the rabbits scampering along the path before her, Granny Rumble-tummy made her way to the fallen tree.

Billy was still dangling by his braces, looking very frightened, but he brightened when he saw the old woman. Then she did something very strange. She spread out the quilt on the ground in front of her, stood back and whistled. There was a sound of fluttering wings and lots of birds flew down and took hold of the quilt in their beaks. They flew with it until they were hovering just below Billy. Then a bright little woodpecker landed on the fallen tree. He began to peck at the twig which held Billy's braces. ''Peck, peck, peck.'' Then down fell Billy on to the waiting quilt and the birds carried him to safety.

Now that he was safely back on firm ground, Billy thanked Granny Rumbletummy for rescuing him and explained that he had been on his way to see her. "Come along then," the kind old woman said. "While I'm making up the medicine for Poppy and Sam you can have a nice drink of my home-made camomile tea. I think you need something after your adventure!" Later that afternoon Billy made his way home, carrying a large jug of Granny Rumbletummy's Special Cold Cure. And this time, you can be sure that he went over the proper bridge!

RAINBOW'S END